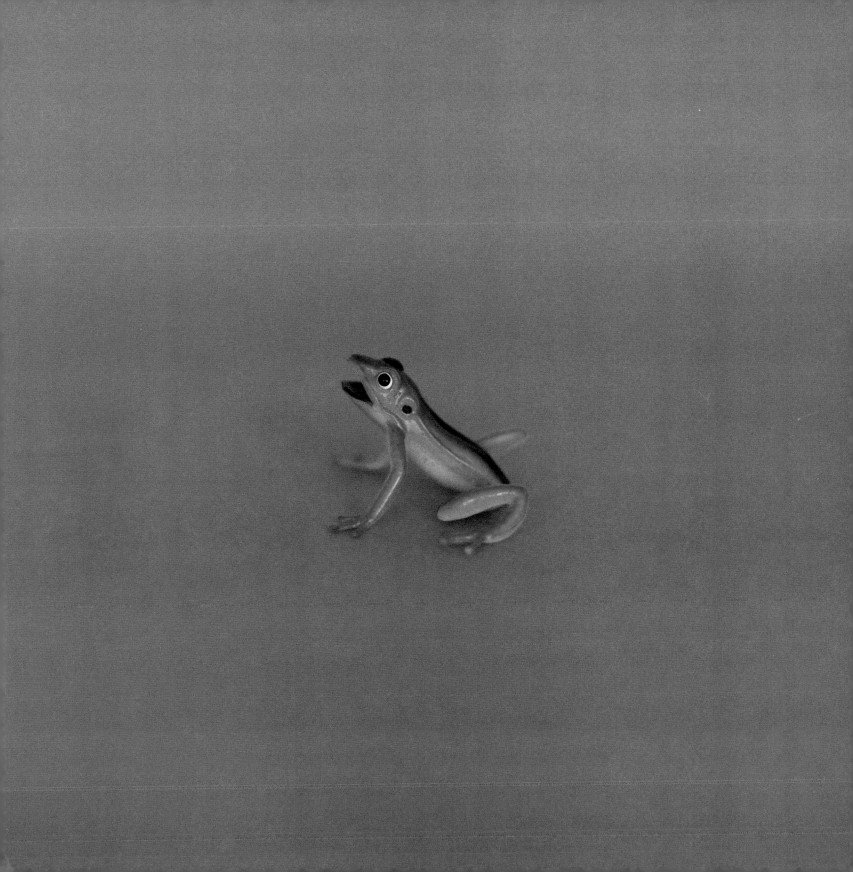

my b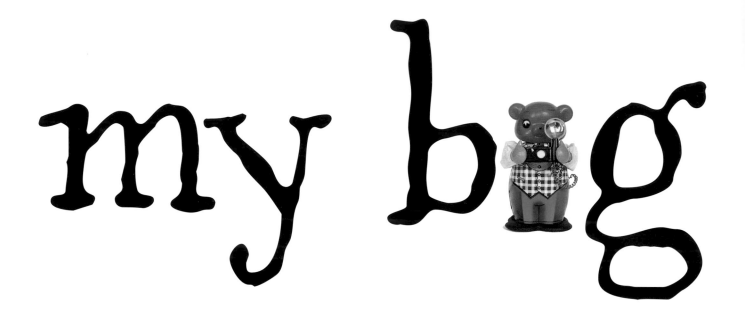g

brother

by Valorie Fisher

POCKET BOOKS

LONDON

ACKNOWLEDGMENTS

Thanks to Karen Hatt, Matt Mitler, Theresa Urbano, Henry Horenstein, and the most patient of dogs, Beanie, for their help in creating this book. And special thanks to Anne Schwartz, Lee Wade, and my husband, David, for their generous enthusiasm.

POCKET
BOOKS

First published in Great Britain in 2002 by Simon & Schuster UK Ltd,
Africa House, 64-78 Kingsway, London WC2B 6AH

Originally published in 2002 by Atheneum Books for Young Readers,
an imprint of Simon & Schuster Children's Publishing Division, New York

This edition first published in 2004 by Pocket Books

A CIP catalogue record for this book is available from the
British Library upon request

Book design by Lee Wade
The text for this book is set in Aunt Mildred

ISBN 0743462122

Printed in China

1 3 5 7 9 10 8 6 4 2

For Aidan and Olive

This is my
big brother.

Everyone makes a fuss over how big I am, but my brother is REALLY big.

He can do the most amazing things.

He has a very
important job,

and some very
funny friends.

Still, he always finds time to play with me.

My big brother
feeds me,

and I feed my
big brother.

My big brother
makes the best music.

I like to sing along.

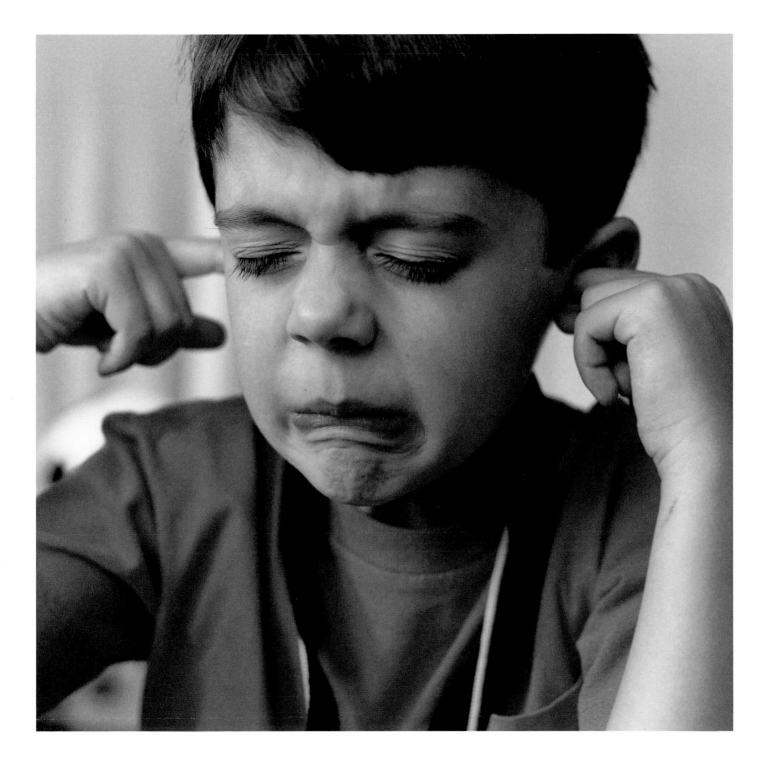

He tells me
he is training
for the circus.

Sometimes I can't find him anywhere,

and then like

magic he appears.

I love my

big brother,

and he loves me.